Little Cliff and the Cold Place

CLIFTON L. TAULBERT · paintings by E. B. LEWIS

DIAL BOOKS FOR YOUNG READERS

New York

Published by Dial Books for Young Readers

A division of Penguin Putnam Inc.

345 Hudson Street

New York, New York 10014

Designed by Atha Tehon

Text set in Greco Roman with Bernhard Modern punctuation

Printed in Hong Kong on acid-free paper

1 3 5 7 9 10 8 6 4 2

Library of Congress Cataloging-in-Publication Data

Taulbert, Clifton L.

Little Cliff and the cold place/Clifton L. Taulbert; paintings by E. B. Lewis.

p. cm.

Summary: When Little Cliff hears about the cold Arctic in school
and wants to go there, his Poppa Joe finds an ingenious way to satisfy
his curiosity without leaving their small town.

ISBN 0-8037-2558-2

1. Arctic regions—Fiction. 2. Cold—Fiction. I. Lewis, Earl B., ill. II. Title.

PZ7.T2114215 Lg 2002 [E]—dc21 2001028594

The full-color artwork was prepared using watercolors.

Author's Note

*Little Cliff and the Cold Place is set in the 1950's, when the word Eskimo was used
for the people inhabiting the coastal areas of Greenland, Arctic North America, and extreme
northeastern Siberia. In 1977 the Inuit Circumpolar Conference officially adopted Inuit,
which means "the real people," to replace Eskimo.*

For Anne Kathryn Taulbert
C. L. T.

For the passionate teachers who impact our lives
E. B. L.

On the chalkboard in Little Cliff's school was a map of the world. Cliff loved to look at the map and hear about places far from Glen Allan, his small hometown.

Until he had started school, Cliff thought the world ended in Greenville, Mississippi, the grandest place his Poppa Joe had ever taken him. There Little Cliff and Poppa Joe would stand and watch the boats and barges make their way down the great Mississippi River. The water stretched as far as Cliff could see. It seemed to be the end of the world.

Today Miss Maxey told his class about another new place. She pointed to Glen Allan on the map. Then her finger traveled to the top of the map. Miss Maxey said this was a very cold place where boys and girls lived in a land of snow and ice.

In the cold place, children lived in houses made of snow and rode on sleds pulled by dogs. They fished in holes cut in the ice and hardly ever saw the sun. Cliff couldn't imagine life without the bright Delta sun. Mama Pearl had told him that the sun was born in the South. He guessed it didn't get up north much at all.

When Miss Maxey went outside to see if the bus was ready, Cliff walked over to the map and found Glen Allan. Then he stood on his tiptoes and traced the distance to the cold place. "Me and Poppa can drive there," he said to himself.

Miss Maxey returned and rang the bell. School was over for the day. Little Cliff didn't stop to play. He ran straight home.

Mama Pearl was waiting on the front porch. Cliff almost knocked her over, he was so excited. "Mama, Mama, Miss Maxey told us about boys and girls who live just past the big river in a very, very cold place—"

"Wait up, boy, what you carrying on about?" Mama Pearl asked as she gave him her usual loving hug.

"Me and Poppa can go to the cold place. Little boys like me ride on sleds pulled by dogs and live in houses made of snow."

"Houses made of snow? Boy, you outta yore head?"

Little Cliff was jumping up and down. "Miss Maxey showed us the place on the big map, a place called Ark—Ark—"

"Arkansas?" asked Mama Pearl in disbelief.

"No, Ark—shoots, I can't think of it now. But it's not far."

Mama Pearl wanted to laugh, but she thought she'd better not. "Cliffy, it sounds a mighty far piece from here to me, but wait till yore Poppa gits home. He'll know about this place."

Little Cliff went to his favorite chinaberry tree to wait for his great-grandfather. He climbed into a fork of the tree and grabbed a handful of hard yellow "hitting" berries. Cliff liked to hide behind bushes and blow the hard berries at his friends through a rolled-up paper shooter. They would be the perfect gift to give to the boys and girls in the cold place.

At last he heard his Poppa's car pulling into the gravel driveway. He scrambled down from the tree so fast that he sprawled on the ground, his handful of berries going every-where. Little Cliff quickly gathered the berries and stuffed them in his pockets.

Before Poppa Joe could get out of the car, Cliff was at the window, talking so fast, the words ran out of his mouth.

"Poppa, Poppa, I saw the cold place on the map today. Miss Maxey told us about snow houses, no sun, and fish in ice holes."

"Slow down, son, slow down," Poppa Joe said as he opened the car door. "What's all this 'bout snow houses and cold fish?"

Cliff grabbed his Poppa's strong hands and walked up the steps to the front porch. "Boys ride on sleds pulled by dogs," Cliff said. "It's just up north. We can go there."

"You say y'all saw this cold place on the map? *Hmmm,* I believe I know the place," Poppa Joe said as he and Little Cliff walked into the front room where he kept his books.

Poppa Joe put on his reading glasses and pulled out an old book from under the table. Cliff stood by the side of his great-grandfather's chair as Poppa Joe flipped through page after page.

"Well, son, here is the cold place you saw, jest as I thought, the Arctic. Miss May Maxey was right, boy, it's a mighty cold place, and it's a mighty long ways from here."

"But, Poppa, it can't be," Little Cliff pleaded. "I saw it on the wall map. All you gotta do is move yore big finger up north and you right there. It's real close."

"Son, folks can't drive to the Arctic."

"But, Poppa, *pleeease*, I wanna go to the cold place," Cliff said as he began to cry.

Poppa looked very concerned. He never liked to see his little boy crying. Then as Cliff anxiously looked into his face, Poppa Joe began to smile.

"Cliffy, I got jest the idea. We can't go to yore cold place, but we can visit my old friend Jacob Goldstein. He was in the Navy, and I know he's been there. I 'spect he has some pictures."

"Why can't we go, Poppa?"

Poppa Joe walked over to Cliff's picture on the mantel.

He brought the picture to Little Cliff and sat down again.

"Whose picture is this?" Poppa Joe asked.

"It's me, Poppa."

"But now take a good look at yoreself . . . and take a good look at yore picture. You are so much bigger than this small picture."

Little Cliff started to laugh. "I'm a big boy. I go to school."

"So you are, son. And the map Miss Maxey showed y'all was just a little picture, but the real world is mighty big."

Cliff was beginning to understand. "So we can't ever go to the cold place, can we, Poppa?"

"Don't think we can, but here's my idea. I recall Mr. Jacob telling me a long time ago 'bout one of his trips to Alaska, the land of the Eskimo, which is up there in yore cold place. We can go to Mr. Jacob's after supper tomorrow. I've been knowing him since we was boys."

The next evening they drove Poppa's old Buick to Mr. Jacob's house and parked the car by a wire fence covered with honeysuckle vines. Poppa held Little Cliff's hand as they walked to the house.

Poppa knocked. Finally the door creaked open. Old Mr. Jacob stood there.

The men shook hands and Poppa Joe reminded Mr. Jacob that he had seen Little Cliff as a small baby. Then he said, "Jacob, my boy here came home yesterday dead set on me and him driving to the Arctic. Couldn't git him to slow down. He wants to see sleds pulled by dogs and snow houses, and he wants to go tomorrow."

Mr. Jacob laughed out loud as he offered them chairs in his cluttered sitting room. "Joe, I bet I know what happened. The teacher down at the school started it all."

Laughing with him, Poppa Joe said, "You so right. Miss Maxey showed the children a map of the world and got them pretty excited."

"Well, I think I may have what your boy wants to see." Mr. Jacob pulled a scrapbook out of a trunk. "These are pictures I took in Alaska many years ago," he explained, sitting beside Little Cliff and opening the scrapbook. "There you go, son."

There were pictures of people dressed in furs outside their
snow houses, a sled pulled by dogs—even one of Mr. Jacob, fish-
ing through a hole cut in the ice!

Cliff could hardly believe his eyes as old Mr. Jacob took out
a small, heavy winter coat trimmed in fur and held it against
Little Cliff. It was just his size. Cliff tried it on and turned
around and around. Mr. Jacob said, "Joe, yore boy looks just like
the kids in them pictures."

When Poppa Joe looked at his watch, Cliff knew it was close
to bedtime. He took the coat off slowly and thanked Mr. Jacob.

That night, while tucking Cliff into bed, Poppa Joe said, "You know, Cliffy, there's a cold place right here in Glen Allan."

Little Cliff sat straight up in his bed. "Where is it, Poppa? Can we go there tomorrow? It's Saturday."

"We sho' can," Poppa Joe answered. "We gonna go to Brother Cleve's ice house. It's a mighty cold place."

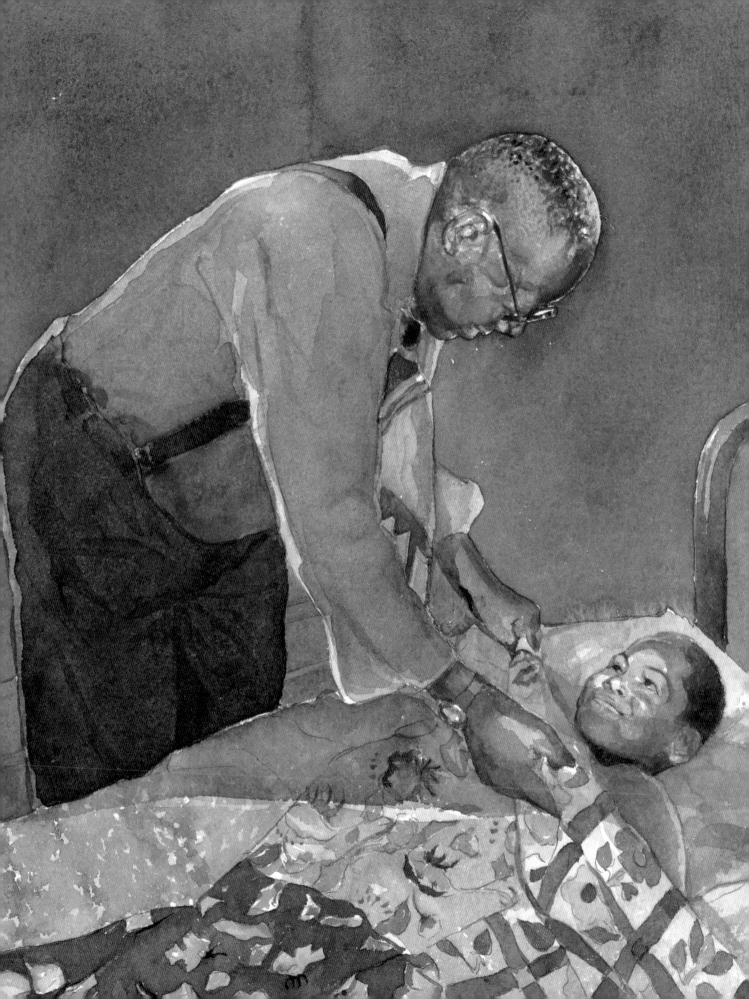

The next day Poppa Joe packed the car with coats, scarves, gloves, boots, socks, an old sweater, and a gray water bucket filled with wet newspaper. Little Cliff climbed in the front seat. He could hardly keep still. He waved at everybody he saw walking along the road and proudly yelled out that he and Poppa Joe were going to the ice house.

Brother Cleve was standing on the front ramp of the ice house when Poppa Joe pulled alongside the building. While the men spoke, Cliff began dragging coats up the wooden steps. "Jest hold it, boy," Poppa Joe said, smiling. "I got a s'prise fer you." Reaching into a paper bag, he pulled out the small parka from Alaska. Little Cliff put on the coat, his chubby face peering out from the fur. He ran to open the heavy door to the blocks of ice. "Wait, boy," Poppa Joe said. "Put on these gloves and pull these thick socks over yore shoes. It's mighty cold in there."

Poppa Joe dressed for the cold also. Brother Cleve just laughed as they took the water bucket and a small quilt into his ice house. Little Cliff had never seen so much ice. They walked down a narrow aisle until they saw a block of ice small enough for them to sit on. Poppa Joe spread the quilt over it. Little Cliff kept blowing his breath and watching it grow cold. Then Poppa Joe reached into the bucket and unwrapped three live fish. Little Cliff's eyes grew wide as he watched them flip in the water bucket. Poppa Joe gave Little Cliff a piece of string with a hook on the end. "Now you can fish, jest like them boys in Alaska," he said. "And you'll be able to tell yore teacher that yore Poppa took you to the cold place after all."

And on Monday morning at the Glen Allen Elementary
School, that is just what Little Cliff did.